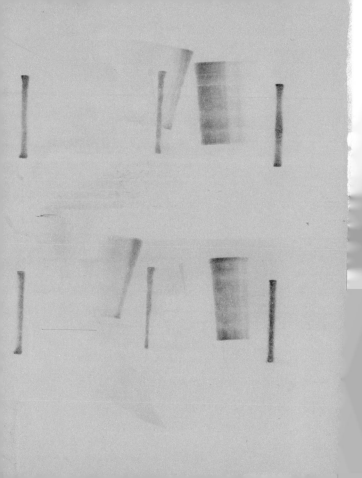

Be
Kind

PEANUTS WISDOM TO CARRY YOU THROUGH

Copyright © 2013 by Peanuts Worldwide LLC
Published by Running Press,
A Member of the Perseus Books Group
All rights reserved under the Pan-American and International
Copyright Conventions

Printed in China

This book may not be reproduced in whole or in part, in any form or by any means, electronic or mechanical, including photocopying, recording, or by any information storage and retrieval system now known or hereafter invented, without written permission from the publisher.

Books published by Running Press are available at special discounts for bulk purchases in the United States by corporations, institutions, and other organizations. For more information, please contact the Special Markets Department at the Perseus Books Group, 2300 Chestnut Street, Suite 200, Philadelphia, PA 19103, or call (800) 810-4145, ext. 5000, or e-mail special.markets@perseusbooks.com.

ISBN 978-0-7624-4862-3
Library of Congress Control Number: 2012954473

9   8   7   6   5   4   3   2   1
Digit on the right indicates the number of this printing

Artwork created by Charles M. Schulz
For Charles M. Schulz Creative Associates: pencils by Vicki Scott,
inks by Paige Braddock, colors by Alexis E. Fajardo
Designed by Rob Williams
Edited by Marlo Scrimizzi
Typography: Archer, Bauer Bodoni, Bemio, Chowderhead, Clare, Clarendon,
Code Light, Copal, FenwayPark, Gill Sans, Helvetica, Legion Slab, Lobster Two,
Neutra, Plantagenet Cherokee

Running Press Book Publishers
2300 Chestnut Street
Philadelphia, PA 19103-4371

Visit us on the web!
www.runningpress.com
www.snoopy.com

Be Kind

PEANUTS WISDOM TO CARRY YOU THROUGH

Based on the comic strip, PEANUTS,
by Charles M. Schulz

RUNNING PRESS
PHILADELPHIA · LONDON

"Happiness is anyone
and anything that's
loved by you."

—*Charlie Brown*

Be
Appreciative

"It's a beautiful little tree, isn't it? It's a shame that we won't be around to see it when it's fully grown."

 —*Linus*

CONSIDERATE

"Tell whoever it is that I can't come to the phone because my dog is sleeping on my lap, and if I get up, I will disturb him."

—*Charlie Brown*

Be
HUMBLE

"I think it's an illusion that a writer needs a fancy studio. A writer doesn't need a place by the ocean or in the mountains. Some of our best books have been written in very humble places."

—*Snoopy*

CARING

Charlie Brown: I'm a great believer in kindness. I think we should be kind not only to other people, but to animals, fish, birds, and all living creatures.

Lucy: I guess you and I have gentle hearts, Charlie Brown. I've always felt sorry for amoebas!

Be Pleasant

Lucy: Do you need help with your homework? I'm good at writing term papers. Go ahead . . . Ask me anything.

Linus: Is "Get Lost" one word or two?

Be
Patient

Be
COOL

SENSITIVE

"You didn't tell me you were going to kill it!"
—Linus

Be Accepting

"I don't know, Marcie. It seems to me you're crabby all the time. I think that's just the way you are.... I tolerate you because I'm the patient, understanding type."

—*Peppermint Patty*

ACCOMMODATING

THOUGHTFUL

"I'm going to send Miss Othmar a wedding present. . . .
A box of eggshells!"

    —*Linus*

"Sometimes I lie awake at night, and I think about the good life I have. I really have no complaints. Then a voice comes to me from out of the dark, 'We appreciate your attitude!'"

—*Charlie Brown*

Be
DEPENDABLE

"I find it hard to believe that my mother raised me to be a tree!"

 —Snoopy

ENDEARING

Lucy: I've just joined a "Neighborhood Watch" program.

Schroeder: Good . . . What are you going to watch?

Lucy: You!

Be
Forgiving

"Yesterday, I threw this stick, but you failed to retrieve it. I, the human being, in our great tradition of forgiveness, will give you, the dog, a second chance."

—Linus

Be PEACEFUL

"Dear Snicker Snack Cereal Company,
I appreciate your offer of one hundred Revolutionary War soldiers for fifteen cents. However, being against violence, I am not sure I want them. Instead, could I please have a set of Peace-Time Civilians?"

—*Charlie Brown*

Be
Hopeful

"Sometimes love letters get stuck way in the back."
  —*Snoopy*

Be
HAPPY

Be
Charming

SUPPORTIVE

Be

A FRIEND

Linus: Do you think a girl could ever fall in love with me across a crowded room?

Charlie Brown: No, you're too short. She'd never see you. Maybe you could stand on a chair.

Be
RESPECTFUL

Peppermint Patty: Good Grief, another rainy day. This is the dorkiest weather I've ever seen!

Marcie: You shouldn't criticize the weather, sir. It's all part of the world we live in.

Be Polite

"It's not polite to land on someone's nose!"
    —*Snoopy*

Be
WELCOMING

Be
HELPFUL

Peppermint Patty: Which would you rather do, hit a home run with the bases loaded or marry the little red-haired girl?

Charlie Brown: Why couldn't I do both?

Peppermint Patty: We live in a real world, Chuck!

Be
Cooperative

"Having your blanket in the wash is like finding out your psychiatrist is gone for the weekend!"

   —*Linus*

Be
Witty

"I want to get a picture of you, sir, in your fishing hat.
We'll call it 'World's Greatest Fisherperson without a Lake.'"

—*Marcie*

Be POSITIVE

"I learned two things in school today. I learned that if you don't watch where you're going, you can get knocked down in the hall. And I also learned that the drinking fountain is out of order! It's not often that you can learn two new things in one day!"

——*Sally*

Be
A ROLE MODEL

Be
Loyal

Be Grateful

"The dentist said I was a good patient and gave me a
free toothbrush. I was hoping for a dog or a bicycle."

—Rerun

Be
ADMIRABLE

"I accept the nomination for the office of school president. If I am elected, I will do away with cap and gown kindergarten graduations and sixth grade dance parties. In my administration children will be children and adults will be adults!"

    —Linus

"We'll quaff a few root beers, and we'll settle our differences like civilized gentlemen."

—*Snoopy*

Be

HANDY

"To those of us with real understanding, dancing is the only pure art form!"

    —*Snoopy*

Be
TERRIFIC

YOURSELF!